Clarence the Copy Cat

Story by
Patricia Lakin

Pictures by
John Manders

A DOUBLEDAY BOOK FOR YOUNG READERS

Clarence's mother and father were the best
mousers Sam's Sandwich Shop had ever had.
They spent all their time catching mice.
Clarence did not. He was a peaceful cat.

He couldn't bear to harm another living creature—
even one that ate the deli meats and scared the customers.
His family tried to change him. But they couldn't.
So Sam sent him away.

Alone in the world, Clarence stuck to his principles.

He would not hurt mice.

But everywhere he went, people wanted him to do just that.

"Scram, you no-mouser!" yelled Gladys of Forever Flowers.

"Scat, cat!" shouted Annie of the Quality Diner.

"Out, you lazy bum!" bellowed Tom of Ye Olde General Store.

Will I ever find a real *home?* Clarence wondered sadly.
He searched up one street and down another.
He sniffed around parking lots and padded along pathways.
But he had no luck.
Exhausted, he collapsed in a small spot of shade.

A man stood in a nearby doorway.

"And whose cat are you?" he asked.

"My own," Clarence meowed softly.

"A stray, by the looks of you," the man said.

He brushed cracker crumbs from his bushy mustache.

"Hmmm. Do I need a cat?" he wondered.

Clarence followed the man into a strange place.
Hundreds of books lined the walls of a big room.
There were tables and chairs in the middle of the floor,
and fluffy cushions lay in a sun-filled window seat.
A big machine whirred, lit up, and spat out paper.

"Welcome to the Barnstable Library," said the man. "I'm Mr. Spanner."
He unwrapped a wedge of cheese and gave it to Clarence.
Clarence purred a deep, satisfied purr.
This place had warm spots for snoozing and many mountains
to climb. But best of all, there were no signs of mice.

There were just friendly people who sat and read books
or carried them in and out of the library.
Clarence watched them come and go each day
as he sat near the door, on top of the copy machine.
Soon Mr. Spanner started calling Clarence Copy Cat.

The two of them grew to depend upon each other.
Clarence helped Mr. Spanner find misplaced books and pencils.
He kept Mr. Spanner company when he had to work late.
And Clarence was the most attentive listener during story time.
In return, Mr. Spanner kept Clarence well read, well fed,
and well petted.
Life was good. Life was very good . . .

. . . until the first bitter cold day of winter.
Clarence smelled him. Then he saw him.
A mouse darted from under the copy machine.
Mr. Spanner saw him, too.
"Get that mouse!" Mr. Spanner called to Clarence.
Clarence's heart sank. He didn't know what to do.

"Come on, Copy Cat!" cried Mr. Spanner.
Clarence didn't move.
He saw Mr. Spanner whirling and twirling, creeping and
crawling all over the library, trying to catch that mouse.
"He's gone!" Mr. Spanner finally panted.
Thank goodness, thought Clarence.

That night, Clarence's past lives flashed before his eyes.
"Out, you lazy bum," "Scram, you no-mouser," and
"Scat, cat!" echoed in his ears.
This time, I can't let myself be kicked out, he decided.
He paced the library floor, trying to think of a plan.

As he rounded the corner of Mr. Spanner's desk,
he noticed that the cheese container wasn't covered.
"Of course!" Clarence meowed triumphantly.
The mouse had been after the cheese.
So Clarence bounded onto the desk and ate every last
cube and crumb.

But the next afternoon, the mouse showed up for story time.
The children squealed.
"Get that mouse!" Mr. Spanner cried.
But Clarence didn't move from his cushion.
He watched Mr. Spanner and the children whirling

and twirling, creeping and crawling around the library,
trying to catch that mouse.
"He's gone!" Mr. Spanner finally gasped.
Then he wagged his finger at Clarence.
"Mice like to eat books, you know."

That night, Clarence couldn't sleep.

He had to save the library books and his home!

He paced the floor, trying to think of another plan.

He was near the copy machine when he saw a tiny hole.

That's it! thought Clarence. *I'll block up every cranny and crack. No mouse will ever be able to crawl in here again.*

Early the next morning,
Mr. Spanner opened the library.
"How did these books get everywhere
except where they belong?" he muttered.
He looked at Clarence, who was perched high above,
in the mystery section. Clarence couldn't explain. And he
couldn't stop Mr. Spanner from removing all his book blockades.

Later that day, Mr. Spanner had just lifted the lid
of the copy machine when he began to shout.
"He's back! Copy Cat, get him!"
The mouse darted behind the library cart.

Clarence didn't move.

Books flew as Mr. Spanner grabbed the broom.

Mr. Spanner twirled. Papers swirled.

Mr. Spanner crept and began to lower the broom.

"STOP!" Clarence yowled.
And, without a plan, he jumped.
He soared through the air.

Mr. Spanner whirled across the room.
Whamp! They collided.

Splunk! Clarence landed, with a big fat belly flop,
right on the copy machine glass!
He tried to get up, but suddenly lights began flashing.
Clarence was blinded by them. They went back and forth,
back and forth beneath him.
Paper flew out of the machine—
one sheet, two, three, four, five . . .

"Gone!" yelled Mr. Spanner.
He picked up Clarence.
"I'm going!" Clarence wailed.
Mr. Spanner put him on the floor.
He gave Clarence's head a pat.
Clarence looked up.
Mr. Spanner wasn't mad!
Clarence wasn't being kicked out.

But what had happened to the mouse?
Clarence peeked under the copy machine.
He jumped when he saw it staring back at him!
It wasn't a mouse.
It was a huge black cat with bulging legs,
an enormous tummy, and whiskers that stuck out like arrows.

It was Clarence. Well, not really Clarence.

It was a large copy of Clarence.

And it was the scariest cat Clarence had ever seen.

It must have been the scariest cat the *mouse* had ever seen, too.

Because that mouse didn't come back. Ever.

Many Saturdays later, after another wonderful story time,
Clarence and Mr. Spanner sat nestled together on the window seat.
They soaked up the last rays of sunlight as they ate their cheese
and crackers.

"I knew I needed a cat like you," said Mr. Spanner.
And Clarence the Copy Cat knew it, too.

For our son, Benjahmin, who is as strongly principled as Clarence.
And with a nod of admiration to John Kovacs, who knows what truly makes a good home.
—P.L.

For Lisa.
—J.M.

A Doubleday Book for Young Readers

Published by
Random House Children's Books
a division of
Random House, Inc.
1540 Broadway, New York, New York 10036
Doubleday and the anchor with dolphin colophon are registered trademarks of Random House, Inc.
Text copyright © 2002 by Patricia Lakin · Illustrations copyright © 2002 by John Manders
Visit us on the Web!
www.randomhouse.com/kids
Educators and librarians, for a variety of teaching tools, visit us at
www.randomhouse.com/teachers

LIBRARY OF CONGRESS CATALOGING-IN-PUBLICATION DATA

Lakin, Pat.
    Clarence the copy cat / by Patricia Lakin ; illustrated by John Manders.
    p. cm.
    Summary: Clarence, a cat who does not want to hurt mice or any other creatures,
does not feel welcome anywhere until he discovers the Barnstable Library.
    ISBN 0-385-32747-1 (trade)   0-385-90854-7 (lib. bdg.)
    [1. Cats—Fiction. 2. Mice—Fiction. 3. Libraries—Fiction.]   I. Manders, John, ill. II. Title.
PZ7.L1586 Cl 2002
[E]—dc21
                                    2001028538

The text of this book is set in 18-point Bodoni Book.
Book design by Trish P. Watts
Manufactured in the United States of America
October 2002
10 9 8 7 6 5 4 3 2 1